MICHAEL
JORDAN

W9-CTF-773

# MICHAEL JORDAN

## Returning Champion

Thomas R. Raber

LERNER
SPORTS
AN IMPRINT OF LERNER PUBLISHING GROUP

LernerSports
An imprint of Lerner Publishing Group
241 First Avenue North
Minneapolis, MN 55401 U.S.A.

Website address: www.lernerbooks.com


LIBRARY OF CONGRESS CATALOGING-IN-PUBLICATION DATA

Raber, Thomas R.
    Michael Jordan : returning champion / by Thomas R. Raber.
        p.    cm.
    Includes index.
    Summary: Examines the life and career of the high-scoring Chicago Bulls player, who made a brief attempt to play minor league baseball in 1994 and returned to basketball with the Washington Wizards in 2001.
        ISBN: 0-8225-0473-1 (pbk. : alk. paper)
        1. Jordan, Michael, 1963—Juvenile literature. 2. Basketball players—United States—Biography—Juvenile literature. [1. Jordan, Michael, 1963–2. Basketball players. 3. African Americans—Biography.] I. Title.
GV884.J67 R33  2002
796.323'092—dc21                                          2001007219

Manufactured in the United States of America
1  2  3  4  5  6  –  JR  –  07  06  05  04  03  02

# Contents

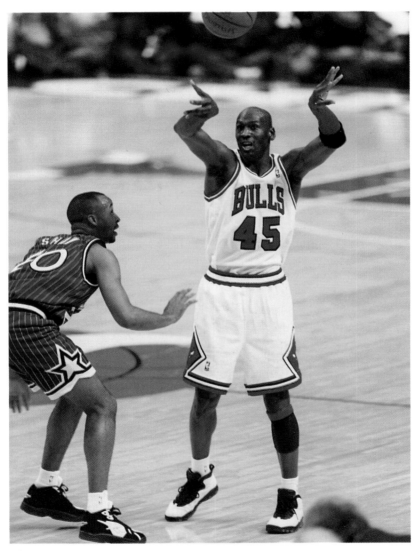

Whenever time was running out and the ball was in Michael's hands, he felt he controlled the game.

# 1

# *The Sweet Sixth*

As the clock ticked away the final minute of Game 6 in the Chicago Bulls' 1998 championship series against the Utah Jazz, Michael Jordan had the ball.

"I feel like I'm in total control," the 6-foot, 6-inch Bulls guard once said. "Whatever's going to happen out there, it's not going to happen until I start it."

If Michael could make something good happen for the Bulls, they would win this game and the title. With about 40 seconds to go, Michael cut a three-point Jazz lead to one.

Then Utah had the ball, but not for long. Michael stole the ball from Karl Malone and raced down the court. "I looked up and I saw 18.5 seconds left," Michael said. "I felt like we couldn't call a timeout. It gives the defense an opportunity to set up. It was a do-or-die situation. I let the time tick to where I had the court right where I wanted to."

Then Michael made a jump shot that swished through with just more than five seconds remaining. "All we had to do was play defense for 5.8 seconds, and I knew we could do that," he said.

They did! The Bulls successfully defended their NBA title and celebrated their sixth National Basketball Association championship in eight years. Michael, Scottie Pippen, and Coach Phil Jackson rejoiced with the Bulls and their fans. The three had been the core of Chicago's successful title drives. As the fans hollered and cheered, many wondered if this was the last game for these three. During the season, Pippen had said he would rather play for another team. Coach Jackson had said he was going to retire. And Michael had told reporters he didn't want to play without his favorite teammate and coach.

With the sixth title in hand, Michael could look back at a season that had as many tense moments as happy ones. For a while, Chicago hadn't looked able to make it past the Eastern Conference finals. The surging Indiana Pacers were eager for a spot in the Finals. Chicago won the first two games of the series, but Reggie Miller and the Pacers won the next two games to even the series.

Determined to show they were still powerful, the Bulls crushed Indiana in Game 5. Then, the Pacers fought back to win Game 6. Michael fell on a play that might have tied the score with five seconds to go.

Never had Michael's team needed seven games to reach the Finals. In the tense Game 7, Michael didn't play one of his best games but he contributed 28 points to the Bulls' 88–83 victory.

Going into the Finals, the Bulls pulled together. Chicago had never lost a Finals series and had beaten the Jazz in the Finals the year before. Still, the Bulls lost the first game of the series.

Chicago went out and won the next three games. One game away from the title, the Bulls were stopped by the Jazz in Game 5. Pippen was hurt for Game 6.

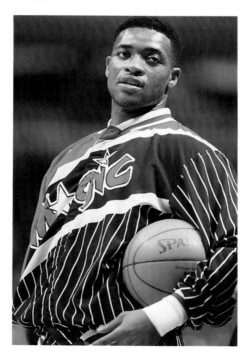

In 1995, Nick Anderson, then with the Orlando Magic, told reporters that Michael wasn't playing as well as he had before retiring. After Michael led the Bulls to the title in 1996, 1997, and 1998, other fans and players disagreed. (Anderson has since been traded to the Memphis Grizzlies.)

Michael earned his fifth Most Valuable Player Award in 1998.

But Michael boosted his performance and scored 45 points, including the game-winning shot.

With the victory came the question: Were the unbeatable Bulls going to break up? Coach Jackson retired almost immediately. Then, the NBA team owners "locked out" the players on July 1, 1998. Owners and the players' union were split over how players should be paid. The owners said the players were asking for too much money and too many benefits in their contracts. The players argued that the owners were making a lot of money and should share the profits. While the two sides argued, the owners refused to trade or sign individual players to contracts.

The 1998–99 season did not start when it was scheduled. Finally, during the first week of January in 1999, the owners and players reached an agreement.

One week later, Michael announced his decision. He was retiring from basketball.

Reporters packed into United Center on January 13, 1999, to hear Michael's announcement. Fans in Chicago, and all over the country, watched TV and listened on their radios.

"Physically I feel fine," Michael said, "but mentally, I just felt like I didn't have the challenges in front of me. It was difficult because you're giving up something that you truly, truly love. My love for the game is very strong. It's hard to give up that love."

It was on that note that Michael Jordan left the game of basketball in 1998. Only three years later, he announced a much-anticipated return. The same reasons that caused Michael to retire were calling him back, to the delight of fans around the world.

Michael in high school

# 2

# *Growth Spurt*

Michael Jordan has played basketball almost as long as he can remember. He was born on February 17, 1963, in Brooklyn, New York. When Michael was a baby, his family moved to Wilmington, North Carolina. Michael's first basketball net was a trash can. At age five, Michael would dunk balls into the can and pretend he was a basketball player.

Soon, he was enjoying the real game. Michael's father built two basketball goals in the family's backyard. "[Basketball] was pure fun," Michael said. "Something everybody in the neighborhood just loved to do."

Michael liked to watch college and pro basketball when he was growing up. His favorite college team was the North Carolina State Wolfpack. Michael also loved playing baseball and football and riding a bike through the woods near his home. The Atlantic

Ocean was only about 3 miles from the Jordans' house. Sometimes Michael went to the beach with his older brothers Ron and Larry, his older sister Delois, and his younger sister Roslyn.

Yet, Michael's youth wasn't always easy. At Laney High School in Wilmington, some boys called Michael "bald head" because of his short hair. "I thought I was ugly, and people made fun of me," Michael said. "They made fun of my close haircuts during the time that everybody else was growing their hair long into Afros. Guys would rub my head and make me mad.

"Then there were my ears. They stuck out. People made fun of my ears and called me names." Eventually, though, Michael became more popular with his classmates. He enjoyed camping and, for a while, played trumpet in the high school band.

Michael's mother, Deloris, worked in the customer service department at a bank. His father, James, supervised workers at an electric plant. Michael often watched his father work around the house and yard. In doing so, Michael picked up a trait that is familiar to most of his fans. "My father used to stick his tongue out when he worked," Michael said. "I took it up and made it a habit."

Michael credits his parents with teaching him how to succeed. "Very early they taught me right from wrong," he said. "You always have to focus in life on what you want to achieve."

Baseball was one of Michael's favorite sports while he was growing up. He's in the middle row, second from right.

Despite his parents' important lessons, Michael sometimes made trouble. He squirmed out of doing errands or bribed his brothers and sisters into doing his chores for him. "I sometimes got into trouble because I didn't look for summer jobs," Michael said. "I didn't obey my parents and didn't do my schoolwork. I clowned around a lot, picking on people and cutting classes."

Michael sometimes struggled in sports, too. Larry often beat Michael in rough games of basketball. Afraid he might not grow tall enough to succeed in the game, Michael sometimes hung from a chin-up bar, trying to stretch himself.

In the ninth grade, at 5 feet, 8 inches tall, Michael dunked a basketball for the first time. By tenth grade, Michael stood 5 feet, 11 inches. He tried out for the varsity basketball team but didn't make the squad. The day he was cut, Michael acted strong in front of his friends. But later, "I cried privately," he admits.

From his sophomore to his junior year, Michael worked hard to improve at basketball. He grew 4½ inches that year and kept growing! Michael made the varsity team his junior year and broke all of Laney High's basketball scoring records. He led the Laney Buccaneers to their first conference championship.

During high school, Michael (front row, second from right) became serious about basketball.

Playing above his competition was part of Michael's game in high school.

Michael was selected as a high school All-America. But he sometimes made mistakes. "I once dribbled [instead of passed] the ball inbounds during a high school championship game, and that cost us the game," he remembers.

In spite of that embarrassing event, many colleges wanted Michael to play basketball for their teams. Michael visited dozens of schools during his senior year. Although he had cheered for North Carolina State while growing up, Michael accepted a scholarship to attend the University of North Carolina at Chapel Hill.

After considering his options, Michael accepted a scholarship to play basketball for the Tar Heels.

Basketball was very important to Michael, but he also wanted a solid education. "I saw the school as a student, not as an athlete," Michael explains. "The University of North Carolina fit my lifestyle." Michael decided to study geography in college.

The North Carolina Tar Heels were a long-standing power in college basketball. Since the Tar Heels had so many talented players, people thought Michael would have to sit on the bench a couple years before he got a chance to play for the team.

But Michael quickly earned a starting spot with the Tar Heels. By March 1982, freshman Michael Jordan had helped his team reach the National Collegiate Athletic Association (NCAA) championship game. Michael was just 19. He and his teammates were up against a powerful team from Georgetown University.

There were 15 seconds left in the game, and Georgetown led by one point. With time running out, Michael launched a shot. He was 18 feet from the basket. The ball went through the hoop.

North Carolina won the game 63–62, and Michael Jordan was a hero. "At the time, that was the biggest shot of my life," Michael said.

During his sophomore season at North Carolina, Michael worked hard to become a more consistent basketball player. He worked with longtime North Carolina coach Dean Smith at improving his defensive skills. At the end of the 1982–1983 season,

Michael was named College Player of the Year by *The Sporting News*.

At the start of his junior year, Michael was trying hard to live up to his reputation as the best college basketball player in the country. But Michael couldn't relax and didn't play well. Finally, before a game against cross-state rival North Carolina State, Michael shaved his head. He was totally bald! Michael wanted to cut away the past and make a fresh start.

The trick worked. Michael bounced back from his slump to lead the powerful Atlantic Coast Conference in scoring that season. He was named the top player in the NCAA for the second straight year.

Michael enjoyed playing college basketball. He was popular on the North Carolina campus. But Michael was also eager to become a professional basketball player. He wondered whether he should pass up his senior season at North Carolina and enter the National Basketball Association (NBA) draft.

After long talks with his parents and with Coach Smith, Michael decided to turn pro after his junior year. He was the third player chosen in the NBA draft that summer. Rather than return to college, Michael would become a member of the Chicago Bulls basketball team. He was determined to finish his bachelor's degree in geography, though. He knew he could play in the pros and still attend college classes in the summer.

Playing for the University of North Carolina, Michael polished his game and drew the attention of basketball fans all over.

Michael was excited about a pro career. He was also honored to be chosen to represent his country as co-captain of the United States Olympic basketball team in 1984. During the Summer Games, held in Los Angeles, California, Michael led his team in scoring and steered the United States to an 8–0 record and an Olympic gold medal.

Before the Olympics, the American team played several practice games against a group of NBA players, including Magic Johnson. When asked to choose the most talented member of the Olympic squad, Johnson did not hesitate. "Michael Jordan," he said. "He's head and shoulders above everyone else."

When the Olympic ceremonies were over, Michael headed for his new home in Chicago. He was set to soar against the pros.

Michael headed to the NBA and began developing his acrobatic style with the Bulls.

# 3

## *Air Time*

Michael Jordan joined the Chicago Bulls only weeks after earning a gold medal in the Olympics. He was used to winning. The Bulls were not a winning basketball team, however. They had not qualified for the NBA playoffs in three years. In seven of the previous nine seasons, the team had lost more games than it had won.

Michael hoped he could change Chicago's fortunes. "When I came to the Bulls, we started from scratch," Michael said. "I vowed we'd make the playoffs every year." Michael stuck to his vow. The Bulls qualified for the playoffs in 1985, and Michael scored an average of 28.2 points per game that season. He led the Bulls in scoring, assists, and steals. He was named NBA Rookie of the Year.

Michael showed early that he was one of the league's most exciting players. He had not been a flashy player in college. But with the Bulls, Michael often had to carry the team. He had to find new ways to break free for the basket. "In the early days, I built up the personality and creativity of my game," Michael said.

The fans took notice. During Michael's first year, home attendance at Bulls games grew by 87 percent. People also crowded into arenas to see Chicago on the road. It wasn't so much the Bulls that interested basketball fans—it was Michael Jordan.

Few players were so much fun to watch. Opposing fans sometimes even booed their own players for fouling Michael on his way to the basket. A foul ruined an opportunity to see Michael dunk the basketball!

Sometimes other basketball players would interrupt their own workouts to watch Michael practice. They marveled at his ability. "There isn't anything he can't do," said Wes Unseld, a former NBA All-Star. "A lot of guys can dunk the ball, but most guys need the whole court to do the fancy stuff. Jordan can do [all] those things with a few steps."

"Nobody has ever played in the air better," said former NBA scoring champion Rick Barry. "He's a once-in-a-lifetime player."

Indeed, Michael seemed to "hang in the air" longer than anyone else. "When I'm up in the air, sometimes I feel like I don't ever have to come down," Michael would say.

Dunks by the high-flying Michael made the highlight films and drew fans to Bulls games.

But even Michael must come back to earth. During the third game of Michael's second professional season, he broke a bone in his foot. He was expected to miss about four weeks of action. But his foot didn't heal as quickly as everyone hoped. Michael missed most of the 1985–1986 season. He watched Bulls games from the bench, sitting next to his crutches.

Michael was miserable. After missing 64 games (more than three-quarters of the season), he was finally allowed back on the court. But team doctors limited his playing time to only seven minutes per half. Gradually, Michael played more and more. By the end of the season, he was playing regularly.

With Michael sitting out much of the year, the Bulls suffered through a 30–52 season and just barely earned a playoff spot. Not surprisingly, the Bulls were eliminated in three straight games by the Boston Celtics. But Michael scored 63 points in one game, a playoff record! He was back—better than ever.

And Michael had money as well as fame. When he first signed with the Bulls, he received a multimillion-dollar contract. He could buy sports cars and pickup trucks, first-class suits and shoes. Because he was so tall and slender, Michael sometimes had a hard time finding clothing that fit well. Now he could have his clothes custom-made.

Michael enjoyed his new wealth, but he didn't live grandly. He didn't hire a housekeeper to clean his apartment. He cleaned it himself. And he didn't distance himself from his fans, friends, and neighbors.

One Halloween night, the Bulls were playing on the road. Michael didn't want the neighborhood kids to think he'd forgotten them. So he left a note on the door of his apartment that read:

> "DEAR KIDS, I'LL BE BACK IN THREE DAYS IF YOU WANT TRICK OR TREAT.
>
> —MICHAEL JORDAN."

Michael didn't forget his commitment to his own education either. As planned, he returned to the University of North Carolina for two summers. He finished his college degree in 1986.

In his spare time, Michael can often be found on a golf course. He first started playing the game in college.

Michael takes a breather during a break in the action.

Michael still felt strong ties to his old school. He wore a pair of North Carolina blue shorts under his Bulls uniform. "I'm not superstitious," Michael said. "But I do consider them to be my lucky charm."

Michael began to meet famous athletes, politicians, and actors. He traveled to many foreign countries. NBA games are televised in other nations, and people recognized Michael everywhere he went. But despite new faces and new opportunities, Michael liked being with his old friends the best.

"They keep my life straight," Michael said. "They are my roots.... True friendships develop over a period of time. That's why I cherish the friendships I had with people before I became famous."

With his foot fully healed, Michael charged into the 1986–1987 season. In the opening game, he scored 50 points against the New York Knicks. He went on to score 3,041 points that year—becoming only the second NBA player to score more than 3,000 points in a season. Basketball legend Wilt Chamberlain had accomplished the same feat 24 years earlier.

Within minutes, though, he's going full bore again—leading his team quickly downcourt.

Michael scored more points that season than his three best teammates combined. In nine straight games, he scored 40 points or more. Two times he scored more than 60 points—again an achievement matched only by Wilt Chamberlain.

Michael also made 236 steals and blocked 125 shots that year. No other player had ever had more than 200 steals and 100 blocked shots in one season. In fact, Michael blocked more shots than 13 NBA centers—some of the tallest players in the league.

Michael continued to shine in the 1987–1988 season. He won the NBA Most Valuable Player award and was named Most Valuable Player of the 1988 All-Star game. He was league scoring champion and was selected as the NBA's Defensive Player of the Year. He again recorded more than 200 steals and 100 blocked shots in a season.

Michael followed his MVP year with more sparkling seasons. Each year he made countless shots in the clutch. Each year he came through in dozens of close finishes.

In a 1989 playoff game, the Bulls trailed the Cleveland Cavaliers with just four seconds left. The Cavaliers assigned four players to cover Michael for the final play. Michael scored the winning basket anyway.

In the following playoff round, the Bulls went up against the Detroit Pistons. Michael made a game-winning basket with three seconds left to play.

Off the court and in media interviews, Michael's friendly demeanor gained him legions of fans.

In September 1989, Michael married Juanita Vanoy. But marriage wasn't the only thing that changed Michael's life. His popularity had spread far beyond the basketball court.

Many big companies wanted Michael to help them advertise their products. Michael promoted a line of sneakers for the Nike shoe company. He even helped design the shoes, which were named "Air Jordan."

Michael began promoting soft drinks, breakfast cereal, cars, and more. Even people who never watched basketball saw Michael on television.

Although he was making millions of dollars as a basketball star, Michael earned far more money—more than $15 million a year—by endorsing products. Michael was astounded by his wealth. "I never imagined I could generate these dollars," he said. "No one could ever have thought about it happening this way."

Yet some people resented all the attention Michael was getting. The Bulls were a team of 12 players. The entire team was improving each year. But some fans and sportswriters gave Michael Jordan all the credit for the Bulls' success.

Others said Michael tried to do too much on the court by himself. Some people thought Michael was too flashy, too confident, and too selfish with the basketball. A great player, they said, helps his teammates play well too.

And Michael didn't always get along well with his teammates. Some Bulls didn't like Michael's showmanship. They resented that he appeared in so many TV commercials. Sometimes Michael criticized his teammates harshly in return. He said certain team members didn't work hard during games.

Some opponents didn't like Michael either. The NBA is full of great athletes. But Michael often received more than his share of praise, while other players were overlooked. Michael would pump his fist after scoring a basket. Some opponents thought Michael was trying to insult them.

Michael's flashy plays sometimes drew criticism from people who thought his game wasn't well rounded.

Another criticism of Michael was that he tried to do too much by himself.

Michael was upset by the jealousy and bad feelings. But he knew that success often comes with a high price tag. "There's always a downside when you're put up on a pedestal," he explained. "Every mistake knocks you off it. You're always a target for people who want to knock you down."

Although many opposing players admitted that Michael had amazing basketball skills, they said the Bulls were a one-man team. Critics were quick to point out that the Bulls had never won an NBA championship.

After years of early playoff exits, Michael longed to celebrate a championship.

# 4

## *Feeling like a Champ*

Michael always took criticism to heart. When people said he was only a scoring machine, Michael stepped up his defense. When critics said he could only dunk, Michael became a brilliant outside shooter. "I don't want anyone to feel that I have a weakness.... If you push me toward something that you think is a weakness, then I will turn that weakness into a strength," Michael said.

By the start of the 1990–1991 season—his seventh in the NBA—Michael was focused on winning a championship. Second-year coach Phil Jackson had been telling Michael that the key to a championship trophy was teamwork. Coach Jackson urged Michael to make sure his teammates were part of the action throughout each game.

Michael did not always score the key basket to win games that year. Sometimes, he would set up one of his teammates for the crucial goal. "I'd rather score 10 points less a game and win 20 more games a year," Michael said. "We have players surrounding [me] that make us an effective basketball team."

Coach Jackson added: "Michael can have a bad game and we can still win. That didn't used to be true."

The Bulls won a team-record 61 games, and Michael led the league in scoring for the fifth year in a row. After losing to the Detroit Pistons two years straight in the Eastern Conference title game, the Bulls finally defeated their archrival to get a shot at the league championship.

Michael was thrilled. "I've been waiting for six years to get to this point," he said. "We're here. We can't let it get away from us."

The last obstacle to a Bulls championship was the Los Angeles Lakers and superstar guard Magic Johnson. The Lakers were back in the Finals for the ninth time since 1980, looking for a sixth championship in 11 years.

The Bulls might have lost some fire when the Lakers won the first game, 93–91. But they fought back in Game 2—a game that is memorable for an incredible shot Michael made. Airborne and heading for a slam dunk, Michael saw a Laker player moving in to block the shot. So instead of dunking, Michael—still airborne—shifted the ball into his other hand and scooped it upward. It bounced softly off the backboard, then passed through the hoop. No one had ever seen a shot like it. The Bulls won the game, 107–86. They went on to win the next three too. Michael Jordan was a winner—and so were the Bulls!

Michael guards Laker Magic Johnson closely during the 1991 NBA Finals.

With his wife, Juanita, at his side, Michael tells reporters how good it feels to win the title. Michael's father, James, is in the background.

Michael was selected as the MVP for the Finals, but he cared more about finally having the trophy. He was so thrilled to have won a championship at last that he broke down in the locker room and wept. He had begun to think the moment might never come. "All those little doubts you have about yourself, you have to put them aside and think positive," he said. "I am gonna win! I am a winner!"

In addition to winning the scoring title and the MVP award, Michael was selected to the league all-defensive team for the fourth straight season. But

Michael was most proud to be a champion—a team champion. "The stigma of being a one-man team is gone," he said.

The Bulls were happy to win a championship. But they also felt they needed to win another title in 1991–1992 to be considered a great team. In recent years the Los Angeles Lakers and the Detroit Pistons had won back-to-back titles.

Winning another title wasn't going to be easy with all the controversy that came Michael's way. During the summer, there was a rumor that Michael was going to snub the Olympic basketball team. Pro players were going to be allowed to play on the U.S. Olympic team for the first time in 1992. A report had come out saying Michael wasn't going to accept an invitation to join this "Dream Team." Another rumor said Michael had cost Detroit's Isiah Thomas a spot on the team.

Then when Michael showed up for the Bulls training camp in the fall, reporters were always asking why he didn't go to the White House with the rest of the team to meet President Bush. Some of Michael's teammates grumbled to reporters about having to attend the ceremony that Michael was allowed to skip.

Adding to Michael's difficulties, a book called *The Jordan Rules* was published early in the season. It told about friction between Michael and his teammates during their title run.

Michael was livid. The book was written by Sam Smith, who covered the Bulls for a Chicago newspaper. Michael had considered him a friend. "When you're on top, some people want to knock you down. I can accept that. But I never thought that it would be someone that I knew, someone that I had spent time with and someone that I had been frank with on a lot of subjects." Instead of talking about how well the Bulls were playing, Michael found himself answering reporters' questions about the book.

Michael's season included even more controversy. In midseason, police found a check from Michael among the belongings of a convicted drug dealer. Later, photocopies of checks signed by Michael were found in the briefcase of a nightclub owner who had been robbed and killed. In both cases, Michael had paid the money for golf bets he had lost.

NBA officials met with Michael to discuss his gambling and the people with whom he had gambled. "It was two-and-a-half hours of like when you're a kid and they find out that you've done something bad in school and the principal calls your family in," Michael told *Chicago Tribune* columnist Bob Greene. "Everyone's there for one reason, which is to talk about you, and you have to sit there and take it." In the end, Michael admitted his mistakes.

Despite the turmoil, the Bulls were playing well. Chicago improved its record from the previous year by winning 67 games. Forward Scottie Pippen had become a star player. Horace Grant was a solid contributor from his power forward position. Michael had another MVP season, averaging 30.1 points per game.

As Scottie Pippen developed into an excellent player, Michael began to feel he didn't have to carry the team.

Michael turns to the sidelines and shrugs after sinking his sixth three-pointer to set a NBA Finals record for first-half scoring.

Even though the Bulls cruised through the regular season, they needed all their resources for the playoffs. The physical New York Knicks pounded on Michael and the other Bulls. Their second-round series went to the full seven games before Chicago pulled out with a win. Then the Bulls fought for another six games to get past the Cleveland Cavaliers in the Eastern Conference finals. Finally, the Bulls were back in the championship series, this time to face the Portland Trailblazers.

Michael started the series with a spectacular performance. He was hitting long-range jumpers as if he were taking practice shots from beneath the basket. By the end of the first half, he had 35 points, including 18 from three-pointers. Then he took on the role of playmaker, finishing with 39 points and 11 assists. The Bulls won Game 1 easily, 122–89. Portland made a contest of the rest of the series, winning Games 2 and 4. But Chicago still came away with the championship. The Bulls sealed the series with an exciting 97–93 win in Game 6 at Chicago.

For Michael the second title was greatly satisfying. After a season full of criticism for things he did off the court, he had helped his team win basketball's ultimate prize. As in 1991, Michael was named the MVP of the Finals. He gained a triple-double that no one else had ever accomplished: league MVP, NBA champ, and Finals MVP in back-to-back seasons.

The Bulls rejoiced with their hometown fans immediately after winning a second NBA championship.

Unlike the year before, when the Bulls had won in Los Angeles, the 1992 victory came in front of the hometown fans. As the Bulls celebrated in their locker room, fans stayed upstairs in the stadium, refusing to leave without another look at the team. The players charged upstairs with their new trophy, climbed onto the scorer's table and danced in front of the fans.

Days after winning the championship, Michael and Scottie Pippen left to train with the national basketball team. They would compete at the Olympics in

Barcelona, Spain, at the end of summer. The Dream Team easily won the gold medal, Michael's second. In eight games, Michael scored 119 points and had 37 steals.

The experience wasn't a smooth one for Michael, though. Before the games began, he said he wouldn't wear the team's warm-up suits because Reebok's logo was on them. A longtime spokesman for Nike, Michael didn't want to look like he was promoting Reebok. Some people said Michael shouldn't let his business deals interfere with the team. Michael compromised by wearing the warm-ups for the medal ceremony, but he covered the Reebok logos with a U.S. flag.

The Dream Team captured the gold medal, and Michael stuck to his principles on the medal stand.

Michael and Scottie didn't have much time off between the Olympics and the start of training camp for the 1992–1993 season. With all of the previous year's starters back, the Bulls were heavily favored to win a third straight NBA title.

When the playoffs finally arrived after the long season, however, the Bulls were underdogs to represent the Eastern Conference in the NBA Finals. The Bulls had finished with a 57–25 record, failing to reach 60 wins for the first time in three years. Along the way, Michael had turned in some awesome performances. He scored more than 50 points in four games. His 32.6 points per game gave him the league lead in scoring for the seventh straight year, which tied him with Wilt Chamberlain for consecutive scoring titles. He also led the league in steals, with 221.

But New York had the best record in the conference and had always played the Bulls tough. Experts picked the Knicks to represent the Eastern Conference in the Finals. Once the playoffs began, the Bulls easily beat Atlanta and Cleveland to advance to the conference championship with the Knicks. New York won the first two games, and the Knicks looked ready to dethrone the defending champs.

During the Knicks series, Michael found himself the center of attention—but not for anything he did on the basketball court. *The New York Times* had reported on a trip Michael, his father, and some friends took to a casino in Atlantic City, New Jersey, the night before the Bulls' second playoff game with the Knicks. Then a former friend of Michael's published a book saying Michael owed him over $1 million for losing bets during their golf outings. Because of the earlier stories about Michael's gambling, some reporters said Michael was addicted to gambling.

After the media flurry about his trip to Atlantic City, Michael stopped talking to reporters so he could concentrate on basketball. In Michael's place, his father spoke. "I talked him into going to Atlantic City," James Jordan told reporters, "and I looked at it as a situation to get away and eat a hamburger. Let's just get away."

When the book was released, Michael denied that he had lost $1 million. "I have played golf with Richard Esquinas [the author of the book] with wagers made between us. Because I did not keep records, I cannot verify how much I won or lost. I can assure you that the level of our wagers was substantially less than the preposterous amounts that have been reported," Michael said. He also said he disliked seeing the gambling reports get more attention than his efforts to win a third NBA championship.

After losing the first two games at Madison Square Garden, Chicago won the next four games. The Bulls earned another trip to the NBA Finals, this time against the Phoenix Suns.

Miffed by the media's in-
trusion into his personal
life, Michael (above) re-
fuses comment for the
throngs of reporters sur-
rounding him as he heads
to practice. But he shares
a joke with good friend
Charles Barkley (right)
during one of their Finals
games.

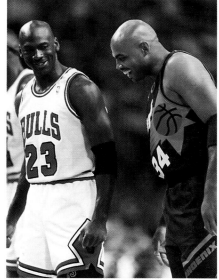

Chicago set the tone for the series by winning Games 1 and 2, both in Phoenix. Game 3 was an exciting contest that Phoenix finally won, 129–121, after three overtime periods. Chicago picked up its third win of the series in Game 4 and needed just one more victory to "three-peat"—that is, to win its third straight NBA championship. The Bulls earned it in Game 6, winning by just one point. Michael scored 33 points, grabbed eight rebounds, and had seven assists. He was again the Finals MVP. During the series he averaged 41 points, a Finals record.

After the third title, there weren't many people left who didn't think Michael was the best basketball player ever. What more could he hope to accomplish? Michael answered that question in his book, *Rare Air,* which was published in 1993. "A fourth title," he wrote. "And then just keep it going."

Michael left the NBA and followed his dream of playing baseball.

# 5

## *The Old Ball Game*

The summer of 1993 was a difficult one for Michael. About a month after celebrating the Bulls' third championship, he was playing golf on the West Coast. There he learned that police had found his father's car in the woods near Fayetteville, North Carolina. Robbers had taken everything of value from the car. Michael worried because no one had seen his father for weeks.

The Jordan family reported James missing. Within a couple of days, police decided a body found in a South Carolina river about two weeks earlier was James Jordan. He had died of a gunshot wound to the chest.

As the police investigated, they thought they knew what happened. After attending a funeral, James drove toward home. Along the way, he stopped to take a nap. Two men saw the expensive car and its sleeping driver. Armed with a gun, they killed James while robbing him. Then they dumped his body into a river across the South Carolina border and drove away in the car. Just a few days after identifying the car as James Jordan's, police arrested two men they had traced through calls made from a cellular phone in the car.

Michael was very sad about his father's death. He was even further disturbed by news reports that suggested James's death was related to Michael's gambling.

Michael and James during a happy time—celebrating the 1992 NBA championship.

Through his agent, Michael criticized the media for the reports: "When James Jordan was murdered, I lost my dad. I also lost my best friend. I am trying to deal with the overwhelming feelings of loss and grief in a way that would make my dad proud. I simply cannot comprehend how others could intentionally pour salt in my open wound by insinuating that faults and mistakes in my life are in some way connected to my father's death."

After the funeral, Michael resumed his routine. He tried to remain positive in spite of the tragedy. "I had a dad for 31 years," he said. "Some children never have their fathers for any years, and I had had mine for almost 31. No one can convince me that I was unlucky."

In October, the Bulls players were returning to Chicago for the start of training camp and looking forward to the 1993–1994 season. Michael was at Comiskey Park one evening, throwing out the first pitch for an American League Championship Series game being played between the Chicago White Sox and the Toronto Blue Jays. In the early innings, a rumor surfaced that Michael was going to retire from basketball.

By the next day, October 6, everyone knew what to expect when Michael spoke at a press conference. In announcing that he was retiring from the NBA after nine seasons, Michael said he had nothing left to prove as a player. He said his father's death wasn't why he was leaving. But he did say that James had encouraged him to retire after the first championship and again after the third. Michael also said he was glad his father had seen his last pro basketball game.

"I think one thing about my father's death is that [I realize] it can be gone and taken away from you at any time," Michael told the roomful of reporters.

With Juanita beside him, Michael laughs during his retirement press conference. He said little about his plans for the future, telling reporters "retire means you can do anything you want."

"There's a lot of family members and friends I haven't seen, because I've been very selfish in my career to get to this point and make sure that I achieved all the dreams I wanted to achieve. Now that I'm here, it's time to be a little bit unselfish in terms of spending more time with my family, my wife, my kids and just get back to a normal life, as close to it as I can."

Fans were stunned. Many past and current NBA players and coaches called Michael's retirement the end of an era. At the press conference, Michael said his leaving would be toughest on the kids who enjoyed watching him play. Even though they were going to miss Michael's moves on the court, a lot of kids understood his decision. Michael closed his press conference by telling reporters they would have to look elsewhere for their stories.

But a few months later, Michael was back in the headlines. Everyone was writing about his new career—as a baseball player!

The stories began in December, when reporters found out Michael was working out at Comiskey Park. Bulls owner Jerry Reinsdorf also owns the White Sox and told Michael he could use the baseball facilities. When reporters asked about the workouts, Michael told them, "I'm just having a good time. I'm just trying to see how good I am."

In January Michael arranged a tryout with the White Sox. He went to Sarasota, Florida, for training camp, where nobody gave him a chance of earning a spot on the club's major league roster. Many people thought Michael shouldn't play baseball.

Other baseball players resented how easily he was able to enter the sport. Most of them had honed their baseball skills for years before getting a tryout. Even some of Michael's fans disliked his new career. They thought he would embarrass himself and hurt his image as the best basketball player ever.

Michael said he didn't care what people said. "[W]hen I'm out there throwing and catching and hitting, I can't even tell you how good it makes me feel. All of a sudden I'm a kid again.... I don't know if I'm good enough, but I have the will to try to do something." Michael spent hours getting hitting advice from the White Sox's batting coach, Walt Hriniak.

Even though many people felt Michael shouldn't be playing baseball, fans flocked to White Sox spring practices and exhibition games to watch him. They cheered wildly when Michael made a play in the outfield, no matter how easy. Michael was used to having thousands of people cheer for him during his basketball days, but the attention bothered him on the baseball field. Fans were paying more attention to him than they were to All-Star players like Frank Thomas and Ozzie Guillen.

Before the end of training camp, White Sox officials decided Michael wasn't ready to play in the major leagues. Instead, they invited him to play for the Birmingham Barons, a minor league team in Alabama. Michael saw the offer as a chance to keep working on his baseball skills and maybe earn a spot on the White Sox roster.

With the Barons, Michael worked harder than anyone else. He usually arrived at the clubhouse before any of the other players to take extra batting practice and to study videotapes of other hitters.

After sliding into a base during a Barons game, Michael looks back to see the umpire's call.

When the season began, Michael was doing well at the plate. He had a 12-game hitting streak and was batting over .300 toward the end of May. Then opposing pitchers discovered that Michael had trouble hitting certain pitches. They would throw only those pitches. Michael's batting average dipped below .200. Still, he kept working hard and finished the season strong. At the end, Michael's average was .202, and he had hit three home runs and driven in 51 runs. Only six players among all the Class AA players in the country had at least 50 runs batted in (RBI) and 30 stolen bases. Michael was one of them.

After the Barons' season ended, Michael accepted a chance to play in an instructional league for baseball's top prospects—the players who showed the most potential for earning spots on a major league roster. He was assigned to the Scottsdale Scorpions of the Arizona Fall League.

Before the fall season began, though, Michael returned to Chicago Stadium to play in Scottie Pippen's charity basketball game. It would be the last game played in the stadium, which was about to be torn down. The Bulls would be playing the 1994–1995 season in the new United Center, built across the street from Chicago Stadium.

The game had the feel of an all-star game—lots of scoring and little defense. Michael finished with 52 points as his team won, 187–150.

Michael drives around former teammate Horace Grant.

With six seconds remaining in the game, Michael headed off the court. When he reached the Bulls logo at the center of the court, he dropped down and planted a kiss on the floor. It was his way of saying good-bye to Chicago Stadium.

With help from Jeffrey and Marcus, Michael raises a banner with his number 23 to the rafters at United Center. Michael's daughter, Jasmine, seems more interested in watching the crowd.

Not long after, Michael began his season with the Scorpions. But he was soon back in Chicago. The Bulls were retiring his number in a glitzy ceremony at the United Center. Money from ticket sales for the ceremony was to be donated to a new Boys and Girls Club that would be named after James Jordan.

Surrounded by his family, Michael watched the unveiling of a statue showing him soaring toward a basket. In the crowning moment of the night, he and his children—Jeffery, Marcus, and Jasmine—raised a banner with the number 23 to the rafters.

A statue of Michael graces the area outside the United Center.

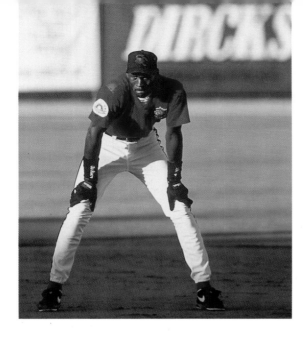

After the retire-
ment festivities,
Michael returned
to Arizona and
his job with the
Scorpions.

The next day, Michael was back in Arizona, playing outfield for the Scorpions. Scottsdale coach Terry Francona, who had also coached Michael at Birmingham, was impressed with Michael's progress. "I'm amazed at how far he's come.... The strides he's already made are really something." Still, Michael had to improve a lot more before he could play in the major leagues. Some people thought he would never make it. "[H]e's got a long, long way to go," said one major league scout. "He's below average in every area. But if he were 25 instead of [almost] 32, there'd be a bidding war to get him."

When the short fall season ended, Michael had hit .252 with eight RBIs. He left hoping to rest after nearly a full year of playing baseball, and he planned to come back for spring training in great baseball shape.

Major league baseball players had gone on strike the previous August, and the strike had lasted through the rest of the season. For the first time since 1904, there was no World Series. When Michael arrived in Sarasota for the White Sox's training camp in 1995, the strike still had not been settled. Team owners said they would start the season on time, even if it meant using replacement players.

Michael said he was coming to camp to prepare for another season in the minor leagues. He would not be a replacement player, because he didn't want to hurt the major league players in their dispute with the owners.

Reporters at spring training saw a difference in Michael right away. He was 20 pounds heavier and had been lifting weights, mostly to strengthen his arms. He was eager to see how much the winter training had improved his hitting.

As practices began, onlookers could tell Michael was hitting the ball better. "This is going to be a big year for him, in terms of finding out what his future in the game is," said Gene Lamont, manager of the White Sox. "The way he hits the ball this year—it sounds different. You can *hear* the difference in his game."

While Michael was happy with his progress, he was disturbed by the labor situation. He felt he was being asked to help break the strike. On March 2, rather than appearing to favor the owners, Michael quit baseball.

The uniform number was different, but Michael seemed his old self when he returned to basketball.

# 6

## *For the Love of the Game*

Almost as soon as Michael left the White Sox, people began saying he would return to the NBA. Michael began to practice with the Bulls. Finally he issued a two-word statement through his agent, David Falk. "I'm back."

When he stepped on the court, Michael was wearing his baseball number—45. He had worn 45 in junior high school but had switched to 23 in high school when his brother Larry wore 45. He also said his father had seen him play his last NBA game wearing 23, and that was the way he wanted to keep it.

Although the Bulls made the playoffs that season, they lost to Orlando in the second round. Michael decided that he didn't feel like his old self in number 45. He switched back to 23 without asking the league's permission. NBA officials fined the Bulls, but Michael kept wearing number 23.

When the 1995–1996 season began, Bulls fans had plenty of reasons to think the team could be better than ever. Michael was in great shape. Scottie Pippen was in peak form. And the team had acquired a top-notch rebounder and defender in Dennis Rodman.

The Bulls met their fans' high expectations. Chicago finished the year with a 72–10 record, the best in NBA history. They cruised through the play-offs, going 11–1, even though Michael had back spasms in the games against New York. The team headed to the finals for the fourth time in six years!

No one gave Seattle much of a chance to defeat the Bulls, but Michael was cautious. "You can't celebrate what we've done so far," he said. "It's nine-tenths done, and you want to complete it so everyone can see the whole picture, starting from the day we lost to Orlando [in the 1995 playoffs]. We're almost there."

The Bulls looked like sure winners. They defeated Seattle by an average of 14 points in the first three games. The Bulls needed one more win to cap their record-breaking season with the NBA championship. Seattle put the celebration on hold by winning Games 4 and 5 before Chicago's 87–75 victory in Game 6.

When the MVP trophy was handed out, Michael received it for the fourth time. "No question about it, Michael is the MVP of this Final," Coach Jackson said. "He was consistently the force and factor."

Michael was mostly just happy to have won the

Even though he was rusty in his first game back, Michael still managed to soar near the hoop.

championship. It came on Father's Day, Michael's first championship without his father. "This was probably the hardest time for me to play basketball," Michael said. "Maybe my mind wasn't geared the way it should have been with my father not being here, but my family and teammates pulled me through it."

In the summer of 1996, Michael became a free agent for the first time in his career. Early in the off-season, he signed a one-year contract with the Bulls, reportedly for $25 million. The new contract made Michael the highest-paid player in NBA history. Even though $25 million was an extraordinary amount of money, few people thought that Michael was being greedy. For years Michael had earned far less money than several other NBA players.

Michael lived up to the costly contract. In April, he reached fifth place on the NBA's all-time scoring list. He was the NBA scoring leader for the ninth time, averaging 29.6 points. He also had 5.9 rebounds and 4.3 assists a game. He helped the Bulls capture their fifth NBA championship in seven years. After the playoffs, Michael re-signed with the Bulls for one more season at an estimated $36 million.

The 1997–1998 season proved to be both thrilling and grueling. Pippen was out for half the season. But when he rejoined Michael and Rodman, the three once again made the Bulls tough to beat.

Michael played well throughout the season and

broke numerous records, becoming the third-highest scorer in NBA history. He won the regular season, All-Star Game, and Finals MVP awards. Michael was only the third person in history to win the regular-season MVP trophy five times. He also broke NBA Hall-of-Famer Kareem Abdul-Jabbar's record of 788 consecutive double-figure-scoring games.

With his impressive on-court performance, Michael's off-court success remained strong. In 1997, Nike launched a new line of Michael Jordan clothes and shoes. That year, Michael also signed a 10-year contract worth roughly $10 million with CBS SportsLine to feature a Michael Jordan website and appear in commercials. During the summer of 1998, Michael's management announced that Michael was no longer seeking new advertising contracts. He had so many commercial sponsors that between his $36 million basketball contract and his endorsements, Michael had made $83 million the previous season.

What does Michael do with all that money? Some of it goes to causes he believes to be important. In 1996, he donated $1 million to the University of North Carolina, his former university, to start the Jordan Institute for Families. Michael hosts an annual celebrity golf tournament to raise money for four Ronald McDonald Houses in North Carolina. He also hosts the Michael Jordan Flight School, a camp that teaches the fundamentals of basketball.

Michael and the Bulls were back in charge!

When the owners locked out the NBA players in July of 1998, Michael sided with his fellow players. Although he did not take an active part in the talks to solve the dispute, he supported his teammates with his presence. Michael did not work out or play basketball while the league was in limbo.

After months of discussions, they finally reached an agreement. A week later, Michael told everyone of his decision. David Stern, the NBA commissioner, was at Michael's press conference. "It's a great day," Stern said, "because the greatest basketball player in the history of the game is getting an opportunity to retire with the grace that described his play."

Michael was 35 when he retired. He said he would enjoy spending more time with his three children. "Being a parent is very challenging," said Michael. "I welcome that challenge and I look forward to it."

NBA fans missed Michael. "He was the greatest player to play the game, period," said Jerry West, executive vice president of the Los Angeles Lakers and also one of the greatest guards in NBA history. "Here was a guy who simply was the best offensive player in the game, the best defensive player in the game, and the best competitor."

"I chose to walk away knowing that I could still play the game," Michael said. "That's exactly the way I wanted to end it." But many people wondered if this was another of Michael's temporary retirements.

Michael stated that he was 99.9 percent sure that he would not return to basketball as a player. But by 2001, no one was quite so certain anymore.

Finally, after several months of hinting, Michael announced the beginning of a new chapter in his career. He signed a two-year contract with the Washington Wizards. "I am returning as a player to the game I love," Michael said. The news came at an unfortunate time. The following day, the United States suffered several devastating terrorist attacks. Michael postponed his press conferences. He also decided to donate his entire salary to the relief efforts. Many fans found Michael's return to the court something to look forward to during the grim days after the attack, but they also wondered what led Michael to this decision.

Michael explained, "I'm not coming back for money, I'm not coming back for the glory. I think I left the game with that, but the challenge is what I truly love." At 38, Michael's age was a source of concern for many. Could he compete at the same level that everyone had come to expect of him? Michael considered the apprehension a challenge.

During his retirement, Michael had kept busy fundraising for charities, playing golf, and raising his kids. And, in January of 2000, Michael had become the president of Basketball Operations for the Washington Wizards. As part of the team's management, Michael played a different role in NBA competition.

Michael takes a shot against the Philadelphia 76ers, challenging four defenders at once.

Michael immediately resumed his place in the spotlight when he announced his return to basketball.

None of these activities, however, could match playing for keeping Michael in shape. To shed the 30 pounds that Michael had added in his three off-court years, he turned to basketball workouts.

These workouts reunited Michael with the game he loved. He wondered if he could still compete with the best in the world. He organized pickup games to gauge his ability and soon started practicing with the Wizards. Although Michael sustained tendinitis in his knee, two cracked ribs, and back spasms, the setbacks didn't sway his determination. "I probably can't take off from the free throw line," he admitted about his dunks, "but I couldn't take off from the free throw line in ['96] when we won the championship."

Michael realized the game offered a new challenge, which he felt it lacked when he retired in 1998. Michael knew he'd have to work hard to meet expectations—his own and those left from his legacy. "While nothing can take away from the past, I am firmly focused on the future and the competitive challenge ahead of me," Michael stated.

Michael approached his return with characteristic confidence. He looked forward to working with a new, young team, a team he helped build from a management position. Michael said, "I am especially excited about the Washington Wizards, and I'm convinced we have the foundation on which to build a playoff-contention team. The opportunity to teach our young players and help them elevate their game to a higher level, and to thank the fans in Washington for their loyalty and support, strongly influenced my decision." Fans immediately returned the favor, boosting season ticket sales.

Excitement continues to surround this returning champion. Watching Michael challenge himself entertained and awed spectators for nearly two decades. Now, despite the apprehensions and expectations, we'll have one more chance to be amazed. "This is a steady process. I'm not in a rush," Michael assured fans. "We'll just keep moving in the right direction." For Michael and for his fans, toward the court is always the right direction.

# CAREER HIGHLIGHTS

### University of North Carolina Tar Heels

| Year | Games | Rebounds | Assists | Points | Average |
|------|-------|----------|---------|--------|---------|
| 1981–1982 | 34 | 149 | 61 | 460 | 13.5 |
| 1982–1983 | 36 | 197 | 56 | 721 | 20.0 |
| 1983–1984 | 31 | 163 | 64 | 607 | 19.6 |
| Totals | 101 | 509 | 181 | 1,788 | 17.7 |

### College Highlights

NCAA championship team, 1982.
Naismith Award winner, 1984.
Wooden Award winner, 1984.

### Chicago Bulls—Regular Season

| Year | Games | Rebounds | Assists | Steals | Blocks | Points | Average |
|------|-------|----------|---------|--------|--------|--------|---------|
| 1984–1985 | 82 | 534 | 481 | 196 | 69 | 2,313 | 28.2 |
| 1985–1986 | 18 | 64 | 53 | 37 | 21 | 408 | 22.7 |
| 1986–1987 | 82 | 430 | 377 | 236 | 125 | 3,041 | 37.1 |
| 1987–1988 | 82 | 449 | 485 | 259 | 131 | 2,868 | 35.0 |
| 1988–1989 | 81 | 652 | 650 | 234 | 65 | 2,633 | 32.5 |
| 1989–1990 | 82 | 565 | 519 | 227 | 54 | 2,753 | 33.6 |
| 1990–1991 | 82 | 492 | 453 | 223 | 83 | 2,580 | 31.5 |
| 1991–1992 | 80 | 511 | 489 | 182 | 75 | 2,404 | 30.1 |
| 1992–1993 | 78 | 522 | 428 | 221 | 61 | 2,541 | 32.6 |
| 1993–1994 | Did not play | | | | | | |
| 1994–1995 | 17 | 117 | 90 | 30 | 13 | 457 | 26.9 |
| 1995–1996 | 82 | 543 | 352 | 180 | 42 | 2,491 | 30.4 |
| 1996–1997 | 82 | 482 | 352 | 140 | 44 | 2,431 | 29.6 |
| 1997–1998 | 82 | 475 | 283 | 141 | 45 | 2,357 | 28.7 |
| Totals | 930 | 5,836 | 5,012 | 2,306 | 828 | 29,277 | 31.5 |

### Chicago Bulls—Playoff Totals

| Years | Games | Rebounds | Assists | Steals | Blocks | Points | Average |
|-------|-------|----------|---------|--------|--------|--------|---------|
| 13 | 179 | 1,152 | 1,022 | 376 | 158 | 5,987 | 33.5 |

### Career Highlights

NBA championship teams, 1991, 1992, 1993, 1996, 1997, 1998.
NBA Finals Most Valuable Player, 1991, 1992, 1993, 1996, 1997, 1998.
NBA Most Valuable Player, 1988, 1991, 1992, 1996, 1998.
NBA Defensive Player of the Year, 1988.
NBA scoring leader, 1987, 1988, 1989, 1990, 1991, 1992, 1993, 1996, 1997, 1998.
NBA steals leader, 1988, 1990, 1993.
All-Star Game Most Valuable Player, 1988, 1996, 1998.
NBA Rookie of the Year, 1984.

# Index

Michael played football during his school days, too.

## ACKNOWLEDGMENTS

Photographs reproduced with permission of: Reuters/Lee Celano/Archive Photos, p. 1; SportsChrome East/West/Rich Kane, pp. 2, 72; Jonathan Daniel/Allsport, pp. 6, 9, 10, 33, 36, 39, 40, 50 (bottom), 52, 61, 62, 63, 64, 66; Cape Fear Museum, Wilmington, N.C., Jordan Collection, pp. 12 (IA3462), 15 (IA3454), 16 (IA3460), 18 (IA3464), 79 (IA3459); Wilmington Star-News, Inc., p. 17; SportsChrome East/West/David L. Johnson, p. 21; SportsChrome East/West/Brian Drake, pp. 22, 27, 28, 29, 31, 34, 43, 46; Allsport/Rick Stewart, p. 25; Reuters/Corbis-Bettmann, pp. 44, 50 (top), 56; Allsport/Mike Powell, p. 47; Reuters/Sue Ogrocki/Archive Photos, p. 54; Allsport/Jim Gund, p. 59; Allsport, p. 69; Reuters/NewMedia, Inc./Corbis, pp. 75, 76.

Cover photographs by © Reuters/NewMedia, Inc./Corbis.